Once Upon a Frame

Library of Congress Cataloging-in-Publication Data

Ulrich, Tom J.
    Once upon a frame / Tom J. Ulrich.
        p. cm.
    Includes index.
    ISBN 0-87842-411-3 (alk. paper) — ISBN 0-87842-412-x (alk. paper)
    1. Wildlife photography. I. Title.

TR729.W54U47 1999
779 .32 092–dc21   99-052322

PRINTED IN HONG KONG BY MANTEC PRODUCTION COMPANY

American Wildlife
P.O. Box 361
West Glacier, Montana 59936

Once Upon a Frame

Tom J. Ulrich

AMERICAN WILDLIFE

WEST GLACIER, MT
1999

Dedicated to my mother and father, Dorothy and Henry Ulrich

Acknowledgments

Several key players helped to mold a pile of photos into the finished product you are holding. A deep thank you for working on grammar, spelling and punctation goes to Julia E. Brewer. She did a great job of smoothing the rough edges and finalizing a manuscript much more pleasing to read. A special thanks has to go to Jeannie Nuckolls and Mountain Press Publishing in Missoula, Montana for answering what seemed to be unlimited questions all pointing me in the right direction. JoAnn Hacker Speelman and Bert Gildart both reviewed a draft of this manuscript, made corrections and provided suggestions to polish the final product. The most important and instrumental person in getting this project off the ground was Deborah Woodley. For her patience in guiding me through computer maneuvers, which were far beyond my previous capabilities, I'm indebted. Again, to all these individuals I give a heartful thanks for helping make a dream come true.

Introduction

While I was employed as a high school biology teacher in Fairfield, Illinois, my brother Mike was stationed in Japan fulfilling a tour in the Navy. Along with a page from a catalogue, I received a letter from him asking if I was interested in a camera. He stated that they were rather inexpensive. I had little interest but said to send one and I would sell it and make some money. Soon after, a camera and several lenses did show up. Instead of selling everything, I started toying with the equipment and eventually had exposed several rolls of film. My first subject was a yellow-shafted flicker cavity nest some seven feet up an old snag. I sat there captivated for hours observing, through the viewfinder of the camera, both adults feeding their young.

It is strange how this one act would eventually carry me to remote corners of the world in pursuit of capturing wildlife on film. These wanderings first started on a national level when every chance I had was spent cruising the West, visiting national parks. The camera became an integral part of these trips as I tried to capture all that beauty on film. One such excursion carried me through Glacier National Park, Montana. While there I was able to spend quality time with mountain goats. Right then, I decided to return someday to photograph them extensively.

After four years of teaching I took an early retirement and limited everything I own to what fit in a van. I headed straight to Glacier Country, and for the next few years that van was home. Much of my time was spent photographing mountain goats and any other critters that came in front of the viewfinder. This allowed me to start building a file of transparencies, many of which became an integral part of this book. Looking to expand my horizons, I started to photograph internationally. I enjoyed going to exciting locations where everything I saw was new.

Many of these photographic opportunities have found their way into this book. You will find them enlightening and entertaining. For me, it is a collection of memories.

Bosque del Apache National Wildlife Refuge is located 100 miles south of Albuquerque, New Mexico. Its location on the Rio Grande River is the winter home for thousands of snow geese and sandhill cranes.

I have made several excursions to this refuge over the years and always seem to come up with something unusual photographically. On one visit I was driving along a dike in the refuge and came across a double-crested cormorant that had just caught a huge black bullhead. For 20 minutes the cormorant tried to choke that bullhead down. It was a great battle as the bullhead kept its pectoral fins extended, keeping the cormorant from working it down its throat. The cormorant never did get that fish down. I rolled down the window, stuck my 700mm out, resting it on a beanbag, and started shooting. With photography, I always find there is a big element of luck at times, and this photo shows it.

I was photographing some birds in central Oregon near La Pine when I noticed a pair of yellow-pine chipmunks skittering about on an uprooted tree stump. I was carrying a cow skull that I often use as a prop. I decided to position that skull near the stump to see what would happen. It was not ten minutes before those two chipmunks had a blast climbing about and investigating that skull. I focused my 500mm telephoto lens from as low an angle as possible with the tripod and started shooting. I call this one "an eye within an eye."

A friend told me about a blue jay nest some four feet off the ground in a cedar tree near Enterprise, Illinois. On my first venture to view any activity about the nest, one of the adults, without any warning, drilled me with its bill straight on top of my head. Ouch, did that hurt! From then on, I've always worn a ball cap for protection, but never again had any problem.

I set up a blind about 11 feet away for my 400mm lens with a small extension tube. I used two strobes set up on light stands about 18 inches away. I preferred to position the strobes as close as possible to the subject as it was much less impact. I used the strobes automatically. By positioning the strobes close, the light was not as bright and the duration they stayed on not as long. The further away a flash is from the subject, the brighter it must be and the longer it has to stay on. The strobes would also recycle faster, allowing me to take more photos each time any adult came in. Both adults came back freely to feed the young. I photographed on several occasions for different stages of development.

I have spent considerable time photographing hummingbirds in flight, using high-speed strobes. I have found that Olson high-speed strobes are the most useful and work very well. With a flash duration somewhere around 1/15,000 of a second, any action is frozen tack-sharp.

Of the dozens of hummingbird species I have caught on film, the snowcap is my favorite. Al Nelson, a super bird photographer from Great Falls, Montana, and I were able to photograph it while visiting the mountains of Costa Rica. Rather small in size for a hummingbird, the snowcap captivated me when I caught glimpses of its prominent white cap as it darted about the vegetation. The female exhibits a much duller appearance as there is no need here to impress the males. Due to the bird's small size, I had to move in to minimum focus with 700mm lens and add a small extension tube.

Peter Dettling, a Swiss photographer/artist and friend, and I drove up to Logan Pass in Glacier National Park early one fall morning. Our goal was to try for a grizzly bear often seen frequenting the pass area. I had tried numerous times before to photograph this bear, but it was always too far away.

We hiked up the Hidden Lake Trail and were just about to the top when we caught sight of the bear. It was far down below us, heading toward the visitor's center. We bolted back down the trail. As we neared the grizzly, it took notice of us and did not seem to mind our presence. At that moment its interest turned to digging for voles and roots. We mounted our cameras with telephoto lenses and started shooting. The light was perfect and I was using my 500mm telephoto to take shot after shot of this beautiful grizzly digging with its rear facing us and its head stuck deep into a hole as it sniffed for voles. All at once it turned around and I clicked off several frames before I noticed a newly caught vole hanging out the front of its mouth.

A pair of violet-green swallows made their home near the top of a snag in Gene Haynes's front yard in Columbia Falls, Montana. I found early morning light was best as it really pulled out the color of this beautiful bird.

My standing 15 feet away at minimum focus with a 700mm lens had little impact as the adults readily came in to feed the young. During all the time I spent there photographing, only once did the male land atop the snag and pose. I quickly pointed the camera in that direction and clicked off several frames.

One mid-November I drove the Alcan highway to the Yukon Territory of Canada. My main destination was Kluane National Park, approximately 140 miles west of Whitehorse. This area offers a great opportunity to spend some time with Dall sheep. At this time of year they are in prime condition for photographing. Their coats are fully furred out, white and sleek, and they are beautiful. The only problem was the stressful climatic conditions. It was bitterly cold. Busting a trail from the valley floor up a steep slope covered with a foot of snow was no fun. The good daylight lasted only a few hours, beginning around 10 a.m. when the sun popped up above a mountain, continuing while it crossed over several mountain tops, and ending when it set behind another mountain about 2 p.m. However, staying in a motel at Haines Junction provided some comfort during the long winter nights.

Having spent much of my life in and around water, I jumped at the possibility to swim with manatees. I was in the vicinity of Crystal River very close to the Gulf Coast of Florida, visiting John Matthews, a former student from a brief teaching career. After a short drive to the town of Crystal River, John and I rented a flat-bottom john boat with motor.

During winter the majority of the manatees migrate from the cold Gulf of Mexico up to Florida's warmer freshwater rivers. Crystal River is an ideal situation with clear water and fairly easy access. Numerous manatee sanctuaries, off limits to humans, are established as part of the river system. Photographic opportunities are presented when the manatees venture out or swim from sanctuary to sanctuary. I used a Nikonos V underwater camera with a 28mm lens. I was as excited about the images I caught on film as I was just being in the water a foot or so away from these gentle creatures.

It was mid afternoon in the Lamar Valley of Yellowstone National Park. At the bottom of a borrow pit alongside the road, I came across the carcass of a yearling elk, apparently struck down by a passing vehicle. Scavengers had already done a thorough job of devouring a major portion of the victim, but none were present when I arrived. I decided to utilize a pull-off some 50 yards further along the road and wait for some hungry critter to show up.

It took 90 minutes of waiting before a pair of coyotes came over a small rise and headed straight for the dead elk. As they took turns pulling at the remains, I stepped out of the truck and slowly made my way down the side of the road. I was not all that excited about shooting down from the road into the borrow pit so I decided to cautiously ease my way down into the pit. Now I could shoot the length of it. It proved to be a good decision.

Eventually one of the coyotes dislodged the head from the remains. With this prize he triumphantly make his way up the slope to my left. He hadn't gone very far when he started to traverse the slope directly above me. I was able to turn my 400mm lens straight up the hill and catch the coyote on film as he was coming across the slope. My first thought was "now there's a coyote trying to get ahead in this world."

On a lake not far from my cabin near Glacier National Park, Montana, I came across a floating red-necked grebe nest. My original intention was to obtain some beautiful portrait shots of the grebes. As I spent more and more time in their presence, I found that I was being accepted by them. I could move as close as I wished. This allowed me to observe various acts of grebe behavior. I started to record this behavior on film with the more ambitious intention of putting together a natural history selection.

Much of my early photography was done from a canoe with a rowing partner. Oftentimes, I leaned way over the side of the canoe, allowing me to get the low angle I often prefer. While I was

attempting this maneuver, my partner sitting in the rear of the canoe leaned very carefully over the other side to keep the canoe from tipping over.

I used a variety of lenses from 15mm very wide angle to 700mm long telephoto. Some of my more close-up shots were done from a float tube while I was wearing chest waders. Eventually, I began wearing a wet suit which was especially helpful when I was working for underwater photos. The biggest challenge I had was trying to get shots of the grebes when they were underwater. Using a 28mm wide angle, I needed the birds in fairly close range to record a nice image. A few times they did come close enough, and I was pleased with the results.

shooting anyway. The great blue heron would have to be back lighted. It was not until my film came back from processing that I saw the back lighting actually enhanced the photograph by bringing out the droplets of water. Amazingly, the heron actually got that frog down.

On one trip to Bosque del Apache National Wildlife Refuge south of Soccorro, New Mexico, I came upon a great blue heron that had nabbed the largest frog I had ever seen. For 20 to 25 minutes the heron wrestled to get that frog into position for swallowing.

Approaching the edge of the water, I could see that photographing the heron was going to be difficult as I was shooting straight into the sun. I set up my tripod with a 700mm lens and started

Probably my most exciting photo excursion was with Bob Stevens. Bob is a retired airline pilot and Alaskan bush pilot with a comparable desire to photograph wildlife. We flew to Mekoryuk on the island of Nunivak in the Bering Sea. Bob knew some of the Inuit there and persuaded two of them to take us out looking for musk oxen.

It was April with winter still hanging on. Snow was everywhere, and it was cold. We traveled 70 miles south of Mekoryuk near the southern edge of the island via dog sled pulled by snowmobile. It was all I could do to keep warm, even though I was wearing a huge parka and was covered by a pile of blankets. The severe cold seemed to have little effect on my guide sitting atop that snow machine and taking the full brunt of that extreme weather. Using a remote hunting cabin for a base, we would venture out to photograph in the best light of the morning and evening. Most of the time I used a 500mm lens so we could set up on tripods near small herds of the animals.

I had never ventured to Olympic National Park in Washington until I received an invitation from wildlife photographer Tom Leeson, who at the time resided in Port Angeles. Every morning we were up early and on Hurricane Ridge in the park. One morning became extra special for me when we came upon a very young fawn. It lay directly in front of us, motionless in the brush. The doe was grazing some 50 yards away. I quickly set up my camera on a tripod with the 55mm macro lens. I took several frames at f32 and ¼ of a second for maximum depth of field. Then I retreated as quickly as possible. From a long way off the both of us waited and watched. It was not very long until the doe casually worked her way back to the brushy area concealing her fawn.

Brent Allen mentioned one day he had a vireo nest on his property and asked if I was interested in photographing it. Since he only lives a few miles away, I felt the opportunity was worth looking into. The nest belonged to a red-eyed vireo and was some seven feet off the ground and readily visible. I set up a platform blind, making it comfortable for me to sit and shoot level to the nest from 13 feet away, minimum focusing distance for my 400mm lens. Due to the heavily wooded canopy, I used two strobes as my main light source. The adults came in often to feed the nestlings as the flashes had little affect on them. The flashes also helped to bring out the red of the eyes.

Way up in the Little Belt Mountains some 50 miles from Great Falls, Montana, lives a rugged individual; her name is Gwen McBride. All winter she supports the avian fauna by putting out sunflower seeds. One species that comes in readily to feast on these tasty morsels is the pine grosbeak. Al Nelson and I are fairly consistent in making an annual pilgrimage to this wintry location to capture grosbeaks on film. As a species, pine grosbeaks tend to be extremely tolerant of people in their territory. No blind is necessary as these birds come in readily while we are in full view, hidden only by the tripods. We utilize a 500 or 700mm lens at minimum focusing distance as they jump from perch to perch on their way down to the seeds.

All excursions to the Galapagos Islands, located off the coast of Ecuador, stop at Seymour Island. The highlight is to view and photograph the frigate birds. Both species, the magnificent and great frigate, nest here. A male in courtship inflates his huge red throat pouch. With this red throat sac fully inflated, he sits atop a possible nesting site. Whenever a receptive female flies over, he sticks out his wings, points his bill straight upwards, and jiggles that red air sac. A trail takes hikers right through a nesting area and occasionally the males are extremely close. A long telephoto will pull them in for a full frame photo and also helps with flight shots. It takes a while to deflate this air sac, so it is common to catch a male in flight with a fully inflated pouch.

A few late winters back in the early 90's, I made special trips south from Montana to the Texas Panhandle to visit Wyman Meinzer. Wyman is a wildlife photographer whose work I really admire. While visiting he was always able to find a Western diamondback rattlesnake just venturing out of its winter den. An expert at handling and controlling these venomous crawlers, he usually got one to hold its ground. This made for great photo opportunities.

Staying just a few inches out of striking range, I prefer to be on my stomach and photograph from ground zero. Oftentimes I actually put the camera on the ground and used it as a tripod. Using a 80-200mm zoom lens from this angle gave the feeling of looking up at the rattler, a result I really liked.

September is a super month to visit the National Bison Range in northwest Montana. It is a great time to experience the pronghorn antelope in rut. I was determined on this trip that I would capture an antelope on film.

Driving along the road that morning, I could not believe it when I came upon this male pronghorn. His horns sported an unbelievably large mass of vegetation. It even hid his eyes. He would walk a few steps and stop, walk a few more steps and stop again and so on. I took numerous exposures with a 400mm lens, watching him until he dropped over a ridge out of sight.

Apparently he had been shadowboxing in the brush to build up his neck muscles and to make his presence known. Some weeds must have gotten stuck on his horns, and as he tried to scrub them off, more weeds got stuck, compounding his problem. Eventually, he must have decided he had better quit while he was behind.

As an invited guest of the Bahamian Field Station on San Salvador island in the Bahamas, I was allowed the opportunity to spend all of one morning on a remote bird island. I could have stayed longer, but there was no relief from the humidity and the sun's heat. By noon I was ready to head back to the field station.

My main goal was to capture the brown booby on film. It was getting late in the nesting season so all eggs had hatched, and the chicks were rather large and in white downy coats. These birds do not see many people so fear is almost nonexistent. With a 500mm lens it was easy to fill the frame. I had no problem capturing individual adults, adults with young, and birds in flight.

Each fall and early winter, Haines, Alaska, plays host to thousands of migrating bald eagles. They congregate along the Chilkat River to feast on the salmon runs. Standing on the bank of the river and looking in every direction, one can observe bald eagles covering the landscape.

Early one morning I came upon a lone adult eagle sitting contentedly on a log just off shore in the river. I slowly climbed out of my van and snapped a few frames. I meticulously scooted down the slope on my rear, taking a few frames each time I stopped and established the tripod. I started with a 700mm lens, but as I neared the water's edge, I dropped to 500mm. Eventually finding myself at land's end, I got the low angle I prefer and filled the frame nicely.

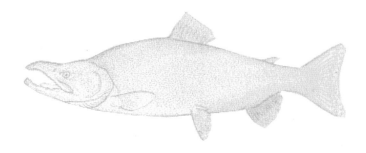

On one of my first adventures to Denali National Park in Alaska, I came upon a huge barren ground caribou in velvet up on a ridge. It was fun to photograph him up on that ridge with blue sky behind. The exciting photography began when he turned and grazed with his head toward me. When he lifted his head, the compression of his antlers and head being closer to me gave a dramatic effect when compressed onto a two-dimensional piece of film. This photo has done well for me because the antlers appear to be so much larger than they really are. Using an 80 to 200mm zoom lens allowed me to compose easily and fill the frame with all caribou.

When I first tried photographing poison arrow frogs in the rain forests of Costa Rica, all I had at the time was a 55 mm macro lens. I found the working distance from lens to subject, in this case the frog, was so short I had to be almost right on top of it. This would often scare the frog away.

My first trip with a 105mm macro made a world of a difference. I was much further away and actually felt that I was not crowding the frog. Also, letting my guide Elston control the frogs for me was instrumental in getting a good photo. Another piece of equipment I found essential was a flash. At first, I mounted it atop the camera on the hot shoe. Due to the close working distance, I eventually connected the flash to the camera with a short pc cord so that I could hold it away from the camera. The final results were a big improvement.

Tasmania is one of my all-time favorite locations to visit. On one excursion to the island, a friend and native Tasmanian, Trevor Westren, made it possible for me to catch a bush flight to a remote area in the southwest part of the island. Trevor works for the Tasmanian Parks and Wildlife Service. The department is studying the rare orange-bellied parrot. It was an opportunity for me to capture this bird on film. This beautiful parrot winters along the southeast edge of Australia and nests in Tasmania. With an annual migration from the south coastal edge of Australia over the Bass Strait, this bird is extremely vulnerable to storms over the open water.

Scientists estimate the total population at less than 100 individuals. A permanent blind set up to study the parrot made my job easy for me. With 700mm and 1000mm lenses, I could fill the frame nicely as the birds came in for seeds. My only intention in this situation was just to record this species.

Bill Sheldon, best friend and aspiring photographer, and I had already spent several days in Jasper national Park, British Columbia, photographing Rocky Mountain bighorn sheep. Toward the end of our stay, we managed to come upon a nice ram sitting atop a rocky ridge. We positioned ourselves so that we were able to compress the mountains far off in the background behind the ram.

I set up on a tripod with an 80-200mm zoom lens mounted on my camera. With this lens I was able to

compose the shot perfectly. As we stood there photographing, a ewe and lamb came up unexpectedly from the far side of the ridge. The ram quickly stood up and walked alongside the ewe. He immediately lifted up his head and performed a beautiful lip curl. Even after the ewe and lamb walked away, the ram held that pose through two complete rolls of film.

One spring I found a loggerhead shrike nest along the road between Fairfield and Burnt Prairie, Illinois. I waited until the hatchlings appeared before photographing them and thereafter spent part of each day at the nest until they fledged two weeks later.

I knew I had something special because this is the smallest bird that eats meat. It has a hooked beak like a hawk or eagle. It catches mice, snakes, and other birds, and feeds the meat to the babies.

One drawback to their physical makeup is that they have weak, skinny feet. They do not have strong talons like hawks or eagles. Therefore, they utilize thorns or barbed wire to impale their prey in order to shred pieces of meat from their victims. Because of all the time spent there, I was tolerated at close distances. I recorded my best photos with a 400mm lens and extension tube at nine feet while they impaled their prey on barbed wire right in front of me.

Bill Sheldon and I canoed out onto a lake in northern Wisconsin one early June evening. At the edge of a small island we came across a common loon sitting tight on a nest. The presence of our canoe did not seem to annoy her as we floated motionless some distance away and exposed some images. I wanted a lower angle so decided to get into the water. Further down the shore of that island I eased into the water and slowly moved closer.

I took a camera mounted with an 80-200mm zoom lens on a tripod and inched my way toward the incubating loon. Under a foot of wood decay there was a hard bottom so I could set the tripod firmly and shoot an inch or so above the water. It gave me the nice low angle I prefer, and I could compose perfectly. I was really happy with the resultsand her for allowing me to get.as close as I needed.

Bob Stevens and I had talked for years about visiting Round Island in Bristol Bay off the coast of Alaska. It is a great location to photograph thousands of walrus. One summer we decided to give it a try and flew into Dillingham. This place is usually the last step before jumping over to the island. We did get grounded there for a few days because of inclement weather. Eventually it cleared somewhat and we rented a jet helicopter for the final flight from Dillingham to Round Island. The island has no accommodations so visitors have to be prepared for primitive camping conditions. Once there I found just about any stretch of rock or beach along the water covered by hauled-out walrus. There truly were thousands of them. I used every lens I carried. It was a fantastic experience as even the weather cooperated for a week. I would have liked to stay longer but the weather was due to change.

Along the Lamar River in Yellowstone National Park one winter, I observed some goldeneye ducks swimming up and back in the rapids. The extremely cold temperatures had most of the river frozen over except for this one open stretch about a hundred yards in length. What really caught my attention was that both Barrow's goldeneye and common goldeneye species were present.

As the shoulder of the road was adjacent to that open stretch of river, I started shooting from there with a 400mm lens and 1.4 teleconverter on a tripod. I had immediately visualized the chance of capturing both goldeneye species in the same frame. They did come close to each other a few times, and I clicked the shutter every instance. In the above photo, the Barrow's goldeneye is on the left. Eventually, I maneuvered myself down the snowy slope to a much lower level so that I could fill some frames nicely with individual birds.

had to be done facing into the setting sun. Longer telephoto lenses in the 700mm range were needed if only one or two individuals were desired in the frame. One particular evening, I was able to record the silhouette of a single spoonbill scratching. I really like the simplicity of this photo with the concentric rings, the inverted reflection, and the rich golden-yellow color.

Back in the embryonic period of my career, each winter I would spend considerable time at J. N. "Ding" Darling National Wildlife Refuge, located along the southwest coast of Florida near Ft. Myers. The avian fauna found here cannot be matched anywhere.

Each evening, visitors to the refuge would meet near the observation tower to witness dozens of roseate spoonbills flying in to roost through the night in the open water. Much of the photography

In the late 1970's I spent a spring in Illinois. During this time I came across an article in the local newspaper about field trips to the Greater Prairie Chicken Sanctuary near Newton. At this time of year the male chickens collect on ceremonial pieces of ground called "leks" and display vocally and visually for females in hopes of mating.

I made a trip to Newton and found Ron Westemeier, employed by the Illinois Natural History Survey, extremely accommodating in allowing me to set up a blind in hopes of working the lek.

Several mornings I entered my blind about 4:00 a.m. in total darkness. Any birds spooked by my presence would quickly return. My patience often wore thin and I would find myself peering through the 400mm lens in the faintest of light, trying to see what my possibilities would be that morning. It was hard not to get excited sitting there waiting for the sun to finally show itself. As it was early in my career, this experience confirmed my desire to do more situations like this.

Many visitors to the Galapagos Islands, which are located some distance off the coast of Ecuador, wish to observe the beautiful and somewhat elusive red-billed tropic bird. On my first excursion to the islands, occasional sightings were possible but always far out of reach for even my strongest lens. It was on my second visit that I had my best chance to record this bird on film. As a group, we had stopped at the edge of a cliff face which dropped straight to the water. We had positioned ourselves here on Hood Island to observe the waved alba-tross nesting toward the center of the island. While standing there, I noticed a few tropic birds flying to their nests, which was below my feet on the side of the cliff face. It only took a few fly-ins before I pointed my camera with an 80-200mm lens and started shooting. I set the camera to auto-focus and attempted to track each bird that came in. It was not until the film came back from processing that I realized the outcome.

I have made several trips to Manuel Antonio National Park, located along the Pacific coast of Costa Rica. Most visitors go there to enjoy the beautiful beaches; I go there to photograph the abundant wildlife. One particular subject is the white-faced capuchins. Everyday a troop of them makes its way through the trees, intent on stealing some visitor's lunch or as much of it as they can get. They seemingly come out of nowhere, grab tasty morsels of food, and are gone to limbs above where the treasures are greedily gobbled down. Trailing them on their pilfering journey offers many opportunities for the photographer. Because the capuchins are continuously in motion, I have found a hand-held 80-200mm zoom lens hand-held works best. Every once in awhile they do slow down, and this is the best chance to capture them on film. It is important to be patient.

Early in my career, I used some chicken wire, electrical conduit, and a piece of plywood to build a fake muskrat hut for use as a blind. To finish the blind, I had to weave cattail reeds, one at a time, into the chicken wire. The whole thing floated atop an inner tube. I remember really having to pinch pennies to purchase a pair of chest waders so that I could venture out into the open water.

My first attempt to use this blind was on a pond near Somers Junction, just south of Kalispell, Montana. The blind concealed me well as I was able to approach a pair of rafting male and female red head ducks. A 300mm lens provided just enough magnification for full frame. I was totally pleased with my handiwork. The blind worked great.

One spring day Al Nelson telephoned me to boast about a grasshopper sparrow he had just photographed some 50 miles south of Great Falls, Montana. That evening I headed for his place so I could try for this bird the next morning. Supposedly, this bird perches atop a fence post and sings its little heart out.

The next morning, following Al's instructions, I pulled off to the side of a back-country road, parked next to a fence post, and waited. In a few minutes that bird appeared. I used my 500mm lens with a small extension tube on a beanbag in the window of my vehicle. The sparrow would leave periodically and land atop other perches, such as a thistle stem out in the field and another fence post further down the row, and then fly back to the post in front of me. At every location he performed his melody of notes, laying claim to his territory. I spent six and a half hours and some seven rolls of film parked there. It was a great photo opportunity and new species for me to catch on film.

Along the edge of the pond in front of my cabin, a family of muskrats had built several feeding platforms on which they stood regularly to munch on the various aquatic veggies they had foraged. As my cabin was under construction at the time, I could monitor their activity from the great vantage point atop the roof while I was pounding nails. From that position, I would sometimes observe up to five individuals collectively scarfing down the vegetation. For several days I took mental notes on when the most activity occurred. It was usually late in the afternoon.

I decided to construct a blind at the water's edge some 12 to 13 feet from the most active platform. I could shoot from ground level for the desired low angle across the water. I left a tripod in place, making it easy to mount my camera with a 400mm lens and to situate myself as quickly as possible. The muskrats performed their task endlessly. My only hindrance was periods of shadowed light caused by trees blocking the sun as it moved across the sky. I was very happy with the results.

Very early one morning I left Gardinar, Montana, the north entrance to Yellostone National Park, and headed north to Livingston. At mile marker 26, I sped past a golden eagle atop a road-kill deer. I had cruised a few more miles down the road when I asked myself why I was in such a hurry. I was just starting a two and one half month road trip. I turned my van around and headed back toward the road kill and the eagle.

Traffic was just about nonexistent so I pulled off on the shoulder of the road and photographed out my window. I braced a 400mm lens on the side mirror, pointing it almost straight ahead of the vehicle. As the sun had still not shown itself above the mountains to the east, I found myself shooting at a low shutter speed. The eagle continued to rip away at the flesh of the deer, filling its crop. I decided to wait patiently some 20 minutes for the sunlight to creep slowly onto my subject. During this wait, I started my engine and moved in a little closer. The eagle tolerated this move and now filled the viewfinder nicely. I did have to watch for a road reflector just out of my field of view immediately to the right of the road kill. I waited until the eagle left and then so did I, having spent a rewarding hour at the side of the road.

Brian Winton, a research student at Oklahoma State University, invited me to share his project involving the study of interior least terns. The study was being conducted at the Great Salt Plains National Wildlife Refuge northwest of Enid, Oklahoma. As this would be a new species for me to get on film, I jumped at the chance.

Photography had to be done early or late as the midday heat was almost unbearable. Brian had located several nest sites so my main concern was to pick the most photogenic one and set up a blind. Except for scattered pieces of driftwood, the terrain was flat salt for miles in every direction. It was the most desolate situation I had ever been in. After a few hours of photographing during several mornings and evenings and having to kill time sitting around during the hottest part of each day, I was ready to leave and head north.

A friend and photographer by the name of Dave Armer and I were visiting in my living room one spring morning. Glancing through the window, I caught movement on the edge of the water at the far side of the pond. I pointed a pair of binoculars in that direction and identified an American bittern patiently stalking aquatic insects and frogs. After observing for a short time and knowing this species is at times somewhat approachable, I asked Dave if he cared to try photographing it.

We slipped the canoe into the water with Dave up front and me controlling the rear. It was a rather slow approach, but eventually we grounded the canoe some 25 to 30 feet from the bittern. I had a tripod with a 500mm lens sitting in front of me. The bird froze its position for four or five minutes but then relaxed and resumed its slow stalking. The bittern was full frame; the only drawback was the overcast conditions. I easily used up a few rolls of film as the bird slowly approached us with all its interest focused on picking off little critters among the aquatic vegetation.

During all my previous trips to Costa Rica, one avian species had always evaded my efforts to capture it on film. The resplendent quetzal is probably the most vibrant, beautiful bird I have ever tried to photograph. I was determined to change my luck so I contacted Marco Saborio, a Costa Rican wildlife photographer and friend. He guided me into the rain forest along the continental divide of Costa Rica. He put me in front of an active cavity nest 30 feet up a tree.

What little ambient light there was came in from the other side of the tree. To help illuminate the darkness at the nest hole, I projected some fill-in flash with a small fresnel lens. All of the photos were taken with either a 500 mm or 700 mm telephoto lens. A few times the male did land away from the nest site, presenting different and exciting photo opportunities. After two days in the rain forest waiting and staring at the nest site, I was ready to move on, but I had finally been able to catch this elusive bird on film.

With the onset of fall in Glacier National Park, weather patterns can change abruptly. This happened one September following a long and hot dry period. A cold front marched in, closing the pass with nearly a foot of snow. Once the weather settled down, the park service worked to open Going-to-the-Sun Road up over Logan Pass. I find the fresh snow at the pass makes a great setting for any wildlife which can be located.

The road was open to an area called Big Bend. Dave Armer and I drove up to the barricade and waited some 30 minutes for the announced noon opening of the road. The sky was heavily clouded and full of energy. As we sat there conversing, the clouds parted, exposing a snowy, sunlit Mt. Canon. I quickly snatched a camera with an 80-200mm zoom lens, jumped from the vehicle, and snapped several frames mostly at the 80mm range. It was a great window of opportunity.

The only mountain parrot in the world can be found on the south island of New Zealand. Visitors to this island must venture toward higher elevations to witness the mountain parrot, called the kea. I found the most accessible and consistent location to photograph this species was at the entrance to the Homer Tunnel leading into Milford Sound.

To attract the kea, all a visitor has to do is pull off onto the side of the road. Within moments, your vehicle will be swarmed by a group of these birds. For some dysfunctional reason, they begin to destroy the vehicle. Anything they can get a hold of with their can opener-like bills is fair game.

Windshield wipers, valve stems on tires, rubber molding around windows, tail lights—all are vulnerable. Any kind of vinyl roof will be peeled away. Some car rental companies have a clause in their contracts that forbids traveling into kea country. These birds tend to be extremely people-tolerant and can be approached with the smaller focal length lenses. I like to use a wide variety of lenses to cover all angles.

When friends come to visit Glacier National Park for the first time, I love to share that first experience of hiking the trail to Hidden Lake Overlook. This is especially true if they come during the first three weeks of August. At this time they have the best chance to experience the peak of wildflower display.

The Hidden Lake Trail starts behind the visitor's center at Logan Pass. The habitat is wide open sub-alpine with widely scattered groups of fir trees. My favorite stretch of this trail lies about ¾ mile from the beginning. It levels out here, and natural water seeps, lined with Lewis monkey flowers and the greenest moss, cross the trail. Photo opportunities are unlimited and any zoom lens in the 28 to 80mm range does wonders.

Walking the road near my cabin early one morning in mid-May, I heard a ruffed grouse drum very loudly and clearly. I peered toward the direction of the noise, and there was the grouse on his log not 25 yards from the road. Each spring the courting male has a favorite fallen log on which he perches in the same location and thrusts his wings forward, compressing air against his breast. The sound carries like a starting lawnmower or chainsaw off in the woods.

This behavior is performed to attract a female for mating.

Since it is heavy forest, only a few directions provided a clear shot toward the log. Not wanting to attract attention from the road, I waited until just before it was getting dark to set up a blind at 500mm range. I entered the blind in total darkness at 4:30 a.m. and waited three hours for the sun to come in. Each night I would pick a different direction from which to photograph. I tried both long and short time exposures. The long exposures produced the more dramatic results.

It is hard not to become excited when a northern cardinal comes into view. I decided on this page to show a variety of cardinal photos I have taken over the years. Each is from a different location taken under various lighting conditions. Any way you photograph a cardinal, you are bound to come out with super results.

Back in the 1970's I spent several falls in Yellowstone National Park just outside Gardiner, Montana, trying to photograph Rocky Mountain bighorn sheep busting heads. At this time of year the big rams come down out of the high country to find out who is the dominant male in the area. I found that I just had to be patient and listen. Once two rams start butting heads, the sound carries a mile. Then it is a scramble to get to them while they are still going at it. Every photographer's dream is to catch two rams fighting on a ridge, in sunshine, with the mountains for a backdrop. Once it happened for me and I was able to record only one sequence with an 80-200mm zoom lens. Apparently they miscalculated and got hung up on each other. This was enough for them to lose interest and go their separate ways.

I have spent considerable time sitting in front of red fox dens in Alaska and Montana. My most memorable experience of a fox den took place in Bowdoin National Wildlife Refuge located toward the eastern end of Montana. Gene Sipe, the refuge manager, said he knew of a fox den not very far from the headquarters area. The den was easy to find and I could actually drive my van just off to the side of the main entrance. For the next one and one half days I sat using my vehicle as a blind,

photographing out the driver window. using Using my 400mm lens, I placed it on a beanbag in the window for stability. The evening of the first day provided the best activity as two of the three fox kits wrestled frequently and freely. I was able to come up with an excellent sequence of play fighting.

On Captiva Island, which lies adjacent to Sanibel Island, Florida, I came across a brown pelican contentedly sitting atop a shell mound. Holding a camera mounted with an 80-200mm zoom lens, I lay down on my stomach and wriggled my way toward my subject, clicking off frames along the way. Eventually, I found myself at 2 1/2 feet, the minimum focus of the lens. To my amazement the bird remained perfectly content. What I did notice is with that lens my depth of field was poor so I switched over to a 28mm wide angle lens and inched my way closer. Making no abrupt movements, I managed to get the lens just six inches away from the tip of the pelican's beak when I took the photo. The wide angle really handled the depth of field much better than the zoom lens.

The Pantanal in southwest Brazil near the Bolivian border has been a rich source of bird photography for me. This vast flood plain in the dry season plays host to a myriad of birds which congregate around water holes teeming with aquatic life. One of the more common predators is the snail kite. This kite is the same species that can be found as far north as the Everglades of Florida. Their prey is snails, which can grow half as large as a man's fist. Adapted with a much longer tip to the upper bill, snail kites have little trouble in dislodging the gastropods from their shells. I had my best luck working them from the window of a vehicle using it as a blind. My camera with a long telephoto lens in the 500mm to 700mm range would rest on a beanbag for stability. I prefer to photograph in early morning or in the evening when the sun is lowering in the sky. This low angle of the sun really seems to bring out the red in their eyes.

in freely with what seemed to be an endless supply of Richardson ground squirrels. When feeding their young, one adult would stand sentinel as the other one offered shredded tasty morsels of squirrel to the hawklets.

At the time I did not have auto-focus setting on my camera. In order to get this photo, I preset the focus manually and just watched from the blind until one of the hawks approached. I was not looking through the camera when the shutter was activated. Again, the element of luck came my way.

George Scotter was instrumental in putting me in front of this ferruginous hawk nest located just across the border in southern Alberta near Cardston. It proved to be an ideal situation as I could set up a blind against a rock face and photograph down toward the nest, using everything from 200mm to 1000mm lenses. The adults came

Bill Sheldon and I had heard Kangaroo Island along the southeast coast of Australia was excellent for a wide variety of wildlife, especially Australian sea lions. We took a late afternoon ferry to the island and spent the night at an auto camp. Bill and I planned to hit the beach early and photograph the sea lions in early morning light. We found the location with no trouble, but the area was not open until 8:00 a.m. Two other people had also arrived, and the four of us waited. By 8:15 no one in command was in sight so the four of us ventured onto the beach and started photographing.

The beach was covered with sea lions. A half hour into getting some great photos, a female ranger in charge appeared on the beach and let us have it for not waiting. We said we had waited and no one had showed up. She insisted she was on time. She was right. While traveling to the beach that morning, we had gone through a 30-minute time chance and did not know it. After she let us off with a light scolding, we went back to photographing. I used just about every lens I carried.

My favorite location to photograph the white-tailed ptarmigan in their winter plumage is the Bow Valley of Banff National Park in Canada. Locating them can be difficult at times because they blend so well with the habitat. Once they are found, these birds prefer not to move far or fast. Another problem is that it is not uncommon for the snow to be waist deep, making it easy to burn up a considerable amount of energy in finding the ptarmigan and then getting into position to photograph them.

Once I am in position, I sit down in the snow with my tripod usually just above the snow level. This gives me the low angle I prefer. Most often I use a 500mm lens. Coming up with the correct exposure can be a challenge. If the bird closes its eye, half the color is gone. I generally overexpose one stop to burn out the muddiness the metered exposure seems to produce. This technique appears to work well in coming up with nice white snow in the photograph.

Anyone visiting the Pantanal from the Brazil side discovers there is only one straight road, a hundred miles long with some 175 bridges to cross. Some of these bridges are in dire need of repair. One time, as Bill Sheldon and I approached one of these rickety old bridges, I noticed a crane hawk sitting toward the edge of one of the planks toward the far end. While we sat there in the vehicle trying to figure out how to attack the situation, the crane hawk diligently began grasping for lizards amongst the crooks and gaps of the bridge, using its long legs to reach in to snatch its prey.

I very slowly eased out of the vehicle first with Bill following. We got down on our rears and cautiously scooted our way down the bridge, being extremely careful of splinters. Each time we stopped, we took several frames. Eventually, with a 500mm lens, we were right on top of that hawk at minimum focus. I was able to click off four or five rolls of film during the approach and before the hawk moved to some pilings at the far end of the bridge, which was not a good setting.

One of the highlights on a visit to the Pantanal of Brazil is to experience hyacinth macaws. Each visit to this huge floodplain near the Bolivian border I contact a local rancher I have come to know who has a sizable wild population of these birds habituating his ranch. The rancher can actually call in these birds. The macaws come flying toward us and make a few circles before landing in a nearby tree, giving me great opportunities for flight shots, hand-holding an 80 to 200mm zoom lens. I also have my 500mm lens ready if they happen to be a little further away or when they take to a tree. I find it a really neat experience just watching them, let alone capturing them on film.

For a few days one early August out in front of my cabin, I noticed a dozen or so cedar waxwings hawking insects on the wing. They flew from natural perches along the edge of the pond and picked off insects in flight.

I set up a tripod and camera with a 700mm lens about 14 to 15 feet away from their favorite perches and sat quietly and motionlessly. The birds landed readily, and I could take numerous photos as they waited patiently for the next insects to fly into range. It was an excellent situation because I could shoot on their level and work a more muted background instead of against the sky. For a few weeks at 4:30 or so every afternoon, they would show up and feast on the flying delicacies. Friend photographers from all over came to capture these beautiful birds on film.

With an entire summer spent in Denali National Park, Alaska, I had many opportunities to photograph Mt. McKinley. The campground at Wonder Lake provided the best possibility for capturing this splendid mountain on film. From this location many photographers venture to the reflecting ponds above Wonder Lake to record near-perfect mirror images of the mountain on the water's surface. I tried this, too, and came up with many acceptable shots.

One evening while camped at Wonder Lake, I paid a visit to Rollie Ostermick, a friend and fellow photographer. He was also a park ranger at that time.

After an evening of catching up on old times, we stepped outside his cabin and viewed McKinley by moonlight. It was 11:00 PM and the glare from the setting sun still lighted one side of the mountain. We quickly retrieved our cameras and tripods, setting up next to the flagpole. My camera sported an 80-200mm zoom lens. For composition I was closer to 80mm and set my camera at auto-exposure. I counted seven seconds while the shutter was open. I was also foresighted enough to take several exposures, which has proven most beneficial when I need extra copies for publication and slide programs.

When I visit Costa Rica, one pastime I love is going out in the darkness of night with a flashlight. It is fun to investigate the foliage, especially the undersides of leaves, to see what critters can be found.

One time I flashed my light on a rather large green katydid. Viewed from the side, it really was not all that exciting. Looking at it head on was another story. From this direction it gave the appearance of being the creature from hell. It was one of the more fearful looking insects I had ever come across. With a camera and 105mm macro lens mounted on a tripod, I moved in slowly to minimum focus. I stopped the lens down to f16 for better depth of field. I was positioned to photograph it head on. Since I was so close, I decided to take the flash off the camera and use it attached by a pc cord. This way I could position the flash near the lens and point it straight at the subject. From the photo you could see the flat lighting produced a rather pleasing shadowless effect.

One of my favorite locations to visit in the Galapagos Islands off Ecuador is South Plaza Island. Except for a forest of cactus, the vegetation is rather low to the ground. Well-marked trails allow visitors to observe one of only two land iguanas found in this archipelago. Much of the time they can be found fairly close to the trail, making it convenient for photographers. On this particular occasion a beautiful specimen was just inches from the edge of the path. I mounted a 20mm wide angle lens to my camera and got down on my side in the trail. This allowed me to place the iguana in the foreground and one of the cacti in the background.

Driving along the California coast, I stopped in Monterey south of San Francisco, hoping to capture sea otters on film. As it turned out, harbor seals were much more productive to work. Next to the Monterey Sea Aquarium is a research station run by one of the California universities. I obtained permission to cross the property so I could get closer to the water's edge and try to photograph some of the seals. When the tide is in, harbor seals will mount rocks just protruding out of the surface of the water. As the tide drops, it becomes a real balancing act for the seals to maintain their positions. It also makes for a great photo opportunity with a 700mm lens.

I heard from a friend in Fairfield, Illinois, about a nest atop a tombstone in the town cemetery. It was a robin nest sitting in a full bouquet of colorful plastic flowers. The ironic feature is that this bouquet sat right on top of a tombstone etched with the name "ROUNTREE."

I waited until the hatchlings appeared and had some size to them. This way they would appear above the flowers when being fed. Using mostly long telephotos, I shot from every direction, trying to utilize as much color in the background as possible. It had to be one of the more colorful settings I have ever experienced for a photo.

I had my best opportunity to photograph desert bighorn sheep in the River Mountains south of Las Vegas. I gave myself a week and spent much of it watching the rear ends of sheep going up the mountains and out of sight. During that week, however, one bit of luck fell my way. One evening I came across a ewe in heat. Sticking right with her was a beautiful specimen of a ram. Since he had other things on his mind, he ignored me. With an 80-200mm zoom I was able to record my best desert bighorn photos, thanks to her.

During one trip to Costa Rica, my guide Elston mentioned a keel-billed toucan that flew into the dining room of a lodge and stole food off the dinner plates. This story aroused my interest immediately as I knew it presented a fantastic photo opportunity. Here was a wild toucan that was tolerant of people.

I checked into the lodge, and for the next two and a half days I worked the toucan. Between meals it could be found somewhere on the grounds of lodge, patiently waiting for the next dinner bell. The grounds provided some beautiful natural settings, but my excitement was really elevated when the toucan sat on the railings of the outdoor dining room, waiting for the opportunity to snatch some morsel of food. This was when I could take the great tight head shots. Of all the photos I took, I favor the larger one to the left.

It is hard not to burn up roll after roll of film on snow geese at Bosque del Apache National Wildlife Refuge in New Mexico. There are so many geese present that unlimited possibilities exist for trying new and exciting ways to photograph them. My favorite time to be out there to photograph is early morning before the sun hits the horizon. The sky at this time reflects wonderful pastels on the water.

Under these very low light conditions I will try long time exposures. By doing this I love the way some of the birds are blurred from movement while others are tack-sharp. Time exposures in the ½ second range work well for me. On a good tripod for stability, a medium telephoto to a long telephoto will give the nice compression feeling to the photo that I desire.

I am often asked what is my favorite bird. The picture that usually forms in my mind is that of the puffin. Although there are three species, two of which can be found along the Pacific Coast and the other along the Atlantic coast, any of them tickle my fancy.

While on a trip to Iceland, I had a super opportunity to view and photograph Atlantic puffins at close range. After talking with some of the Icelandic people who live there, on their advice I took a ferry to the island of Flatey. The ferry I caught left from Stykkisholmur. Once at Flatey it was easy to pay for boat rides out to remote islands dusted with a variety of nesting sea birds. Each species fills its own nesting niche from the vertical cliffs to the flat open areas atop the island. The puffins I was interested in utilize burrows along the top peripheral edge of the cliff to nest. It was easy to sit there and photograph them as they left to feed and return. Much of the time I used my 500mm telephoto lens.

One day in the latter half of August, I made a special trip to Jasper National Park in Canada. I had heard from a friend about a picnic area next to a rocky slope which was home to a group of pika that were extremely tolerant of people.

Sure enough, the photo opportunities were unlimited. The cute little animals, related to rabbits, would scurry atop the rocks, carrying vegetation for haystacks which are tucked away and hidden beneath some of the large boulders. Since these energetic creatures do not hibernate all winter, considerable time and effort are given to these haystacks which help them survive the long winters.

It was fun to stand there pointing a 500mm or 700mm lens supported by a tripod toward the rocky slope. In just a short time I caught on to one of their behavior patterns. As they hurried about their business, they would stop for a moment or two at certain locations. I recorded my best results by fixing the lens on one of these locations. That way, all I had to do was tweak the focus and click the shutter.

One location most bird photographers have visited sometime in their career is the bird rookery at Venice, Florida. A small piece of land completely surrounded by water and heavily overgrown with vegetation, this island makes a great nesting location. Both great egrets and great blue herons in sizable numbers complete their nesting duties here. With some luck and good timing, it is possible to catch some of the birds in courtship display. One time when I had my 500mm telephoto lens mounted to the tripod a great egret sky-pointed, showing off his beautiful green face and filoplumes. I managed to click off several frames to record this neat behavior on film.

There is a location not far from Cuiaba, Brazil, frequented by a group of tufted-eared marmosets. When they are present, it is possible to pull them into fairly close proximity with pieces of banana. If I wished them to pose on a certain limb, I placed a piece of banana there and stood back. An 80-200mm zoom lens, hand held, worked wonderfully well in capturing them on film. I had to be ready as they move quickly and frequently.

While paging through a summer issue of our local weekly newspaper, I came across a feature article about Gene Haynes and osprey, two individuals who loved to fish. The story told how Gene would catch peamouths and suckers which are usually considered trash fish. He would toss out one of these fish, dead, only to watch it get snatched up by an osprey. I immediately asked Gene for permission to tag along, hoping to try my skill in capturing the event on film.

My first attempts were a total waste. I was trying to focus manually, and the bird came in way too fast to follow it. I even tried focusing on the fish and putting the shutter button down with the motor drive on as the bird neared. The results usually were an osprey head coming into the frame or a tail going out of the frame. There would be nothing in the middle where it was needed. On another attempt I went to an auto-focus camera, but it was not fast enough to track the bird as it came in.

Success came when I finally purchased a top-of-the-line autofocus Nikon camera to handle this situation and quickly became extremely pleased with the results. Every time I photographed the osprey, I was hand-holding an 80-200mm zooms lens and wide-open aperature at f2.8.

My favorite time to work the birds was in the morning back light. Sometimes the fish would start to sink, and the osprey would plunge up to two feet, trying to retrieve that fish. This was great for photography. Water would spray everywhere as the bird took flight, really adding to the action. It turned out to be a fantastic opportunity.

ravine and adjacent to a waterfall. It was far from being an ideal photographic situation, but it was accessible. Due to the extremely low light condition, I projected two strobes full power at the nest site and photographed with a 700mm lens wide open. Periodically I returned to Johnson Canyon just to work that nest and record the different stages of chick development. I was happy to finally record this elusive species on film.

I was producing the photos for a Canadian bird book with author George Scotter. He insisted I come up with as many photos of the birds as possible. One species I desperately needed was the black swift. Following his lead, I got in touch with someone from Canadian Parks and Wildlife. This individual personally showed me a black swift nest in Johnson Canyon, Banff National Park. The nest was located 28 feet across a steep

There are two locations on the north island of New Zealand to view Australian gannets. One is in close proximity to Aukland, the capital, and tall cyclone fences limit photography. The fences are totally understandable with all the people traffic that goes by there. I found Cape Kidnappers, the other location, ideal for photographic opportunities. The area is remote and I can usually position myself a few feet away from the nesting gannets. With birds coming and going continuously, any number of lenses work fine. I used everything from a 20mm wide-angle lens to my 500mm telephoto for tight head shots. Most of the flight shots were done with an 80-200mm zoom, tracking as the birds flew toward me on a prevailing offshore breeze.

I love to visit Yellowstone National Park in early October after the hordes of summer tourists have gone home. Then it is a pleasure to be in the park. The elk are past the rut, but they are still there and as beautiful as ever. In the fall the weather can change for the worst at any moment, and it did on this visit. A fierce storm came in from the west one night. The next morning it was blowing snow and the temperature had dropped to five above zero. I figured if the elk can be out in such unpleasant conditions, so could I. Wanting to keep the dampness from destroying my more expensive telephoto lens, I opted to go with a smaller 80-200mm zoom. It was super in helping me to compose the shots.

The first year I put corn out in my pond for the ducks, I had three male and two female wood ducks come in. Other species of ducks—mallard and assorted teal—came in as well, but my interest fell upon the woodies. In each of the following years the number of wood ducks steadily increased. When I had 11 males and nine females, I decided to set up a blind and find out if I could work them.

Since my pond is only 50 yards in front of my cabin and evening light is best, I could wait and pick nights that were ideal. I photographed from an angle as low as possible. I also placed perches at strategic locations out in the water for them to utilize for resting or just hanging out. The photo opportunities were far better than I ever could have imagined.

When I first moved to Glacier country in northwest Montana, I spent considerable time observing and photographing mountain goats. My fascination, I am sure, had something to do with the fact that no other mammal lives higher in elevation than the mountain goat. Although I enjoy seeing them at any time of year, my favorite season to photograph them is the fall when they have acquired their new winter coats and are stunning. They have eight inches of fur and an eight inch beard.

As snow invades the high country, Going-to-the-Sun Road usually closes in stages to motorized vehicles. It is open to biking and hiking. I will climb over the gate blocking passage and peddle up the road on my mountain bike until I hit snow on the road or see a mountain goat I can climb to and photograph. Much of the time it is just me and the mountain goats, and we have the best view in the house. I can work my way in fairly close and use my 80-200mm zoom lens, which is great in helping me compose the shots. I get really excited when I find them up in the cliffs. Sometimes I have no idea where they put their feet. Just as I took the above photo, the goat leaped to his next toe hold and actually jumped out of my focus plane.

Doug Steele, a super Canadian videographer and close friend, had spent considerable time and energy working on a beaver film. One segment consisted of filming beavers inside their lodge. He gave me the opportunity to try photographing stills inside the same lodge.

The beaver lodge Doug filmed was constructed on the bank of a lake north of Edmonton, Alberta. A tunnel he had dug in the earth gave access to a small opening through which to view the living chamber of the lodge. Doug is a considerably smaller-framed individual so for me the tunnel was a tight fit as I inched my way to that window of photographic opportunity. Surrounded by the smell of fresh dirt, I actually felt like an earthworm. The opening did not present much room in which to work. I had to shine a light on the family of sleeping beavers so I could focus. On my first attempt I tried a 55mm macro lens and soon discovered I had too much magnification. Only part of a beaver fit in the frame. I found hand holding the camera with a 28mm wide angle lens was ideal. I also used a single flash mounted to the hotshoe of the camera as my artificial light source. I had no idea how the photos would appear. Coming out into the light of day sure was a great feeling.

Helen Cruickshank and I first crossed tracks back in the mid 70's at Bowdoin National Wildlife Refuge, Montana. Helen and her husband Allen had been pioneers in bird photography. Now a widow, Helen and I became good friends as both of us enjoyed photographing birds. Several springs our paths would cross as we roamed the back roads of Bowdoin. Each time she would invite me down to photograph at her home in Cocoa Beach, Florida.

One winter while touring the state of Florida I took her up on that invitation. Several bird feeders, birdbaths, and water trickles landscaped her backyard. A myriad of bird species came in, but one caught my attention. A half dozen or so pairs of painted buntings came in for millet. I set up a blind about 11 feet from a perch near the millet feeder. I used a 400mm lens with a short extension tube. I also set up two strobes some 20 inches from the perch. I ended up with some great photographs of painted buntings.

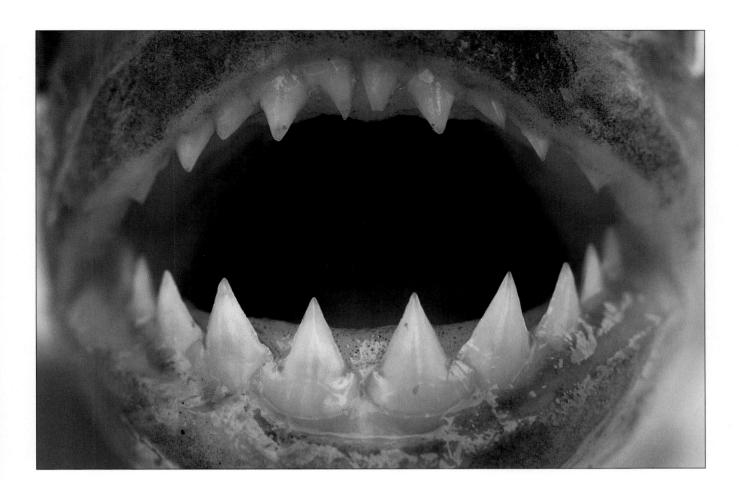

During one visit to the Pantanal of Brazil, I asked Joe, my driver, to catch me the largest piranha he could. I had pictured in my mind a close-up photo of just piranha teeth. It was not long when he came up with one heck of a large specimen. I set up my tripod and camera. Mounted to the camera, I had my 105mm macro lens set somewhat close to minimum focus. I held the piranha in my hand with its mouth open. I moved my hand in toward the front of the lens until I could see the teeth in focus. At that moment I clicked the shutter. To help with depth of field I had the aperture stopped down to about f-11. It looked great through the camera so I was excited to see the results on film.

The most accessible and economical location to view polar bears in the wild is Churchill, Manitoba. There is a reversal here in that the bears dig dens down to the permafrost each summer and sleep. Usually in October they awake, leave their dens, and congregate along the shores of Hudson Bay. They wait patiently for the bay to freeze so they can go out on the ice and feed on seals all winter.

I had a chance to spend eight days in Churchill in late October and early November. Most of my shooting was done from a Tracker vehicle. The roof slides back, making it possible to stand up and shoot, braced on the vehicle about seven feet above the ground. It was no trouble to photograph portraits of bears including tight head shots.

On the last day, two hours before heading back to Churchill, our vehicle was parked near a pair of young males just milling about. Three other Tundra Buggies were also there, but they soon left the area. It was not long after their departure that these two

bears stood up and danced with each other. One bear was about seven feet tall and the other was about nine feet tall.

I had a 400mm lens on and with the motor drive of the camera I quickly used up the roll of film. Bobby McDonald, who traveled along to see polar bears, handed me another camera body, and I quickly mounted it to the 400mm lens and kept shooting. In a short time the film in that second camera was exposed, and Bobby handed me a third camera body. I added the lens and started shooting again. After the film in the third camera was exposed, all I could do was stick my hands in my armpits because I had lost feeling in my fingers. It was -15° F with a 25 mph wind putting the wind chill at -65° F. Even though the bears play-fought awhile longer, I could not change film as my fingers were useless. As everything happened so fast, I don't remember much of what I saw through the camera, but I was extremely pleased with the results.

I had seen a brown pelican photo like the one above many years ago and always wanted to improve on it. During one visit along the southern California coast near La Jolla, the opportunity presented itself. A small group of these birds, their bills tucked under their wings, was resting on the rocks.

Slowly I scooted closer with a 700mm lens mounted on the camera. The pelicans were quite content with just holding their positions. Eventually I could drop my lens magnification to 500mm. I had all the time I needed to choose my subject and compose the photograph. What intrigues me the most about this photo is the feather pattern that drops down to the bottom of the photograph.

Early one morning Steve Ochs, an art professor, and I tried out a used sea kayak he had just purchased at a garage sale. We were on the backwaters of a fairly large lake without much open water near Magnolia, Arkansas. We had to weave between tree snags and fallen logs the whole time. While we were cruising along, occasional piles of aquatic vegetation caught my eye. These piles closely resembled the feeding platforms I have seen used by muskrats further north. I asked Steve if we could park a short distance from one of the platforms and just wait. In only a few minutes, several nutria climbed atop the mound and started to sun bathe. I did not have my camera at the time but convinced Steve to bring me back out early the next day.

When we returned to the lake the next morning, I was able to position my tripod right in front of me on the kayak. It was mounted with a 500mm lens. Steve, seated in the back of the kayak, paddled slowly toward the group and held us steady anytime I needed. Taking our time, we eventually floated into minimum focusing distance. I took everything from long telephoto habitat shots to close-up head shots.

I made a special trip to Mono Lake, California, to photograph the Williamson's sapsucker. I had always dreamed of photographing this bird. It was a new species for me, and one of the last woodpecker species of North America for me to get on film. Danny Malloory, a California based photographer, was extremely instrumental in helping me locate this bird.

During this same trip in a campground along the road heading toward Yosemite National Park, I found the cavity nest of a red-breasted sapsucker. The nest hole was only seven feet up in the trunk of a quaking aspen tree, making it a great photo opportunity. I started some distance from the cavity hole and eventually moved into minimum focus of 10 or 11 feet with my 500mm lens and extension tube. Both adults came back and forth freely to feed their young, giving me numerous chances to film them. This is my last woodpecker species to get on film for North America.

For the past several years, a pair of great gray owls has nested annually just south of Canyon Junction in Yellowstone National Park. Each year the adults and young provide ample opportunities to be photographed. This species is fairly tolerant of people, and any lens in the 700mm range will usually do the job.

One September afternoon while I was visiting the park, I spent a good six hours in the presence of a great gray. It would fly from perch to perch, spending extended periods of time surveying the surrounding area for unsuspecting rodents. Photo opportunities were unlimited, but one time I was especially excited when it landed on a rustic old snag. I did not waste time trying to position myself any closer to the owl. I established the tripod and shot, taking no chances that the bird would move before I could get it on film. It was a fortunate decision because I had only clicked off six exposures before it was gone, flying off into the deeper recesses of the forest.

A photographer friend and I were on the road near an area called Primrose in Denali National Park, Alaska, working a grizzly bear. It was late August and the fall foliage was at its peak for color. The light was perfect, and we were going crazy as this bear would not pick its head up from browsing. Minutes seemed like hours as the bear would not lift its head even for a moment. I was about at the end of my chain when down the road came a park service garbage truck. It pulled alongside our vehicle, and the driver paused to view the scene. Luckily, the evening breeze was at our back and carried the sweet scent of garbage toward our subject. In less than 15 seconds, the grizzly pointed its nose to the air, and I clicked off two shots.

During the first hours of daylight, I worked several huge bull elephant seals and their harems. I was located on the Peninsula of Valdes along the coast of Argentina. As the cool morning air warmed, the activity of the seals slowed down. I found myself shifting among groups along the beach, looking for any behavior as these huge pinnipeds became more and more lethargic with the rise in temperature.

On one venture across the sand, my attention was caught by a loud roar coming from the direction of the open water. Two dominant males had met and were at battle. Luckily, I had my 500 mm lens mounted on a tripod, which I was carrying over my shoulder. Unluckily, I was shooting right toward the rising sun. All I had to do was set my tripod to the ground and starting shooting. Due to the sun's reflection on the water, coming up with a correct exposure was trying. To this day I have no idea what I did with camera settings. One and a half rolls of film went through the camera, and I was pleased with just about all the photos.

Of the three bluebirds found in North America, my favorite has to be the western species. The dark azure blue of the male in sunshine jumps out and grabs my attention. One of my favorite haunts to pursue this magnificent bird is near Perma, Montana. It prefers these rocky, open woodlands with scattered conifers. Western bluebirds are happy to utilize wooden nest boxes which some caring individual has spent considerable time and energy mounting along the fence rows bordering the roadways.

My most productive technique for photographing the bluebirds is to pull alongside an active box, stick a 500mm or 700mm lens out the window, resting it on a beanbag, and start shooting. Both the male and female come in freely to feed the young, making unlimited opportunities to film them.

Back in the late 1970's, I was touring Yellowstone National Park in November. Most of the roads in the park were still open as winter had yet to set in. Every morning was frosty cold; the skies were clear blue. Up early and heading south out of Mammoth at the north end of the park, I arrived at the turnoff to Sheep Eater Cliffs as the sun came in. There was a really heavy frost in a small field along the Gibbon River. Looking toward the sun, I saw that the frost sparkles were a myriad of rainbow colors. I quickly mounted my camera and 400mm lens on my tripod. I positioned myself down low at the edge of the field so that I could compress as many of those sparkles as possible onto the two dimensional plane of film. Although I have been in Yellowstone many fall seasons since, I have never been able to find those same conditions again.

On Kangaroo Island off the southeast coast of Australia, Bill Sheldon and I had hopes of photographing a koala. We had heard the possibility might present itself, but every koala we came across was high up in a eucalyptus tree and not picturesque at all. After three disappointing days trying to photograph a koala and coming up empty-handed, we switched our attention in another direction. There was a chance to try for a platypus inhabiting a water hole a mile hike into the bush.

Late one afternoon we packed up our photo equipment and took off into the forest. Not two minutes and no more than 150 yards from the vehicle, we were astonished to see a koala walking on the ground. We were both caught totally off guard. It was a scramble to procure cameras and lenses, which were tucked away in our backpacks. The 80-200mm zoom lens worked wonderfully as the koala would occasionally stop to sit a spell, giving me ample opportunities to compose the shots.

On one of my fall trips to the Chilkat River near Haines, Alaska, I glimpsed a bald eagle soaring far off in the distance. At the time I had my 500mm telephoto lens mounted to the tripod as I was trying to work eagles which were flying at a much closer range. While watching that eagle soar, I was not long in noticing the spectacular backdrop of mountains. I quickly pointed the camera and lens in that direction and took a shot. I like to think the combination of mountains and wildlife produces a timeless effect.

One late winter Jan Wassink, super photographer and friend, invited me to photograph a black bear sleeping in its den. The area was not far from his home in Kalispell, Montana. We had to make our way several hundred yards up a forested slope to the den; the opening was under the root of a huge pine tree. Having entered the den before, Jan knew that the hole sloped down and made a hard right turn into the sleeping chamber. He would hold my legs to keep me from sliding all the way in. I crawled on my stomach, twisted to the right, and stopped once I sensed the opening to the chamber. At first it was black as night, but as my eyes acclimated, the faintest of light revealed the outline of a bear some three or four feet in front of me. I had preset the focus at four feet. With a 28mm wide angle lens and a flash mounted atop the camera, I started shooting. After several exposures I could hear some rustling ahead of me. I took a few more shots and started kicking to be pulled out. It wasn't until the processed film was returned that I could see the bear had opened its eyes.

The trail I have most often hiked in Glacier National Park is called the Hidden Lake Trail. It starts behind the visitor's center at Logan Pass and climbs up to the Continental Divide between Mt. Clements and Mt. Reynolds. Right near the top where the trail levels out after coming through some trees, a small creek cuts across the trail. On one hike in that vicinity I noticed two Columbian ground squirrels feeding vigorously on the local vegetation.

Suddenly one took off running, leaped the creek, and bolted into its burrow. I figured the second would soon do the same. I quickly set up my 500mm lens on a tripod and focused on a rock at the edge of the creek where the first squirrel had leaped from. As I watched, sure enough, the second ran for the rock. I was not looking through the camera, but as the squirrel hit that rock I pushed the shutter button down. I was really pleased with the result.

Much of my photography takes place early in the morning or in the evening. Animal activity is usually at its peak during these times. As a result, I have witnessed many beautiful sunrises and sunsets. I try to record as many of them as possible.

This sunrise took place in the Pantanal of Brazil. I had arrived at this location solely for the purpose of putting the Jabiru stork nest in the photo in silhouette. In a situation like this, I prefer to bracket settings. I will shoot the photo at multiple settings so that at least one should come out to my liking. Of all the photos taken, I like this one because of the pastels.

During a side trip from the island of Trinidad, near the coast of Venezuela, Bill Sheldon and I visited the island of Tobago. A local avid bird watcher indicated an area where we might photograph some rufous-tailed jacamars. The area turned out to be a not-so-well-used backcountry road that seemed to go nowhere.

Bill and I hiked up and down the road several times, attempting to follow an occasional jacamar we came across. Each time the bird would be hunting insects on the wing. We each sported 700mm lenses. Due to the low light conditions, I mounted a flash to the camera hot shoe to add some fill-in. In order to project the light out 20 feet, I used a fresnel lens mounted to the flash. We did have one good sequence when a bird stayed put long enough for us to focus and click off several frames. I was pleased with the results of several hours spent on that road.

Not very far from where I reside, there is a boggy, swampy area. One spring while skirting the edge of it, I jumped a common snipe off her nest. I could see four golden spotted eggs tightly clustered all pointing toward the center of the nest. I set up a blind, and each day I moved it in a little closer to the nest. Finally, the blind was some 11 feet away, minimum focusing distance for my 400mm lens with a small extension ring.

The morning that I noticed the first crack in an egg, I entered the blind. I spent the next six and one half hours sitting there until all four hatchlings showed up. Once hatching was complete, the snipe took two of the young and left from the right side of the nest. Eventually, she came back for the two that had remained at the back of the nest. According to what I have read, each parent raises two young independent of the other.

This bicycle photo came about because I entered a photo contest. The task was to photograph a bicycle or part of a bicycle with no people in the photo. I wanted to try something different and had this photo in my mind. All I had to do was find a location, the right lighting and a bicycle.

Finding the bicycle turned out to be the hardest of the three. It was getting close to the deadline. I went to a park near the location where I planned to take the shot. I actually sat down in a bike path and waited for someone on a bike to pedal by. It was close to 25 minutes before I could see, off in the distance, a person approaching on a bike. I jumped up and started waving my hands as he bore down on me. He stopped and I said, "Hey, buddy, I need to take a picture of your bicycle." He replied, "No problem."

I positioned his bike below an overpass. I was able to set it perfectly upright by putting a pebble under the kickstand. Thankfully, there was no wind. I ran up on the overpass and leaned way over the side so I could shoot straight down at the bike. He, in turn, stayed down below, watching so no vehicles would come along and wipe out his bike. Everything fell into place, and I was extremely pleased with the results.

The most stable and consistent part of my life for the last 12 years has to be my pal and companion "Bud." His proper name is Charles "Bud" Ulrich. He came into my life through a radio show called *The Trading Post.* An ad announcing "free golden retriever puppies" caught my attention. The ad occurred about Labor Day so I called the number given and indicated an interest in coming by the next day about noon to check out the pups. The voice on the other end of the phone stated, "I'll be at work--if you want one, take one."

The next day I drove to Kalispell, Montana. As I turned the corner to the address given in the ad, I heard a dog yelping. I parked the van, got out, and peered over the fence, spotting two small puppies in a makeshift pen. One was dark colored and the source of the yelping as it jumped up on its hind legs. The other, much lighter in color, just sat there and looked dumb. I did not want a yelper so I grabbed the dumb-looking one and took him out of the pen. He seemed happy and showed an interest in liking me. His ears and feet were huge; thankfully, several months later he finally grew into them.

I put him in the van, which I realized later was a big mistake. I did not let him get used to it enough and consequently ingrained in him a dislike for traveling and being in vehicles.

When we arrived home I let him sniff and investigate inside for awhile. Then I took him outside away from the trailer in which I was living in at the time. I peed and he peed, and from the first day on he was house broken.

He grew up a typical kid, doing typical things kids do. He took skindiving and downhill-skiing lessons. I lived through his episodes of love, ear piercing, and the yuppie years. We established a regular exercise and diet program which eventually consisted of walking thousands of miles down winding roads and eating two square meals a day. In return, his loyalty was relentless just like the billions of hairballs collected off the rug over the years. I could not have asked for a better pal.

Index